Josh and T.J.

By Marcie Heller Aboff
Illustrated by Meredith Johnson

Modern Curriculum Press
Parsippany, New Jersey

Cover and book design by Stephen Barth

Modern Curriculum Press
An imprint of Pearson Learning
299 Jefferson Road, P.O. Box 480
Parsippany, NJ 07054-0480

www.pearsonlearning.com

1-800-321-3106

ISBN 0-7652-2164-0

2 3 4 5 6 7 8 9 10 11 MA 07 06 05 04 03 02 01

Modern
Curriculum
Press

Contents

To Jason, Jeffrey, and Alissa:
my ‘Premium Flash’ source

Chapter 1
T.J. Moves Away

This had been the worst week of my life. My very best friend in the whole world moved away. T.J. and I had known each other forever. We lived right next door to each other, and we played together practically every day. Now he was gone.

On Saturday my mom called me into the kitchen. She had just brought in the mail. "This letter is for you," she said, handing me a blue envelope with my name on it. I tore open the envelope. It was a letter from T.J.!

July 15

Dear Josh,

Hi! Well, it's been one whole week since we moved to our new house. I hate it here!

We drove almost three hours before we got to the new house. It's a creepy place! All of my stuff is in boxes, and there's no one to play with.

My parents keep saying I should be happy now that I have my own bedroom and we live in a bigger house. No way! I would share a bedroom with my bratty little brother Kyle for my whole life if I could stay back home with you.

Write soon!!!

Your best friend,

T.J.

T.J. sounded as miserable as I was. Every time I passed his old house, I had to remember I just couldn't ring the doorbell and wait for him to run out. My mom kept telling me I should play with my other friends. I tried to, but T.J. had always been a part of our group, so things just weren't the same. It felt like there was a big empty space inside me ever since T.J. moved away.

After I finished reading the letter, my mom said, "Since it's Saturday, let's go to the pool."

"All right," I said and went to get my stuff. When I came back downstairs, my mom asked me about the letter.

I smiled. "It's from T.J.," I told her.

"How does he like his new house?" she asked.

"He doesn't like it at all. He never should have moved!" I replied.

"Sometimes it takes a while to adjust to a new home," my mother said. "I'm sure he'll like it more once he gets settled and has a chance to meet some people at his new school."

Because it was such a hot day, the town pool was very crowded. It seemed as if the whole neighborhood was there. I saw some kids from my school, Darren and Carly, over by the diving board. I could even hear Darren ordering everyone around, just as he always did.

I was already walking toward the diving board when my mother stopped and began talking to some people I didn't know, although they looked a little familiar. Then I remembered. They were our new neighbors, the people who had moved into T.J's house.

My mom waved for me to come back. She called, "I want you to meet someone."

When I got to where my mom was standing, she said, "Josh, I'd like you to meet Mr. and Mrs. Walker and Scott and Amanda. Scott is the same age as you." Two kids sat near Mr. and Mrs. Walker, a girl and a boy.

Amanda said, "Hi." She sounded friendly, but she looked like she was a few years older than me. Then Scott looked up. "Hi," he said quietly.

"Hi," I said back. I started to walk away again, but my mother stopped me. She gave me a look, but she didn't say anything else.

"It's nice to meet you," I added.

Then I left and went over to Darren and Carly. As I walked away, I heard my mom and Mrs. Walker talking about the neighborhood and how nice it was to have a pool so close by.

I didn't see Scott or his family for the rest of the afternoon. They must have left the pool after lunchtime, which was fine with me.

I didn't really want to get to know the new neighbors. I felt a little angry that they had moved into T.J.'s house. I knew that was silly because they didn't have anything to do with the reason T.J. moved, but I still felt that way.

After dinner that night, I wrote T.J. a letter.

July 18

Dear T.J.,

Hi! I was really glad to get your letter today. I guess it will take some time to get used to your new house. I don't think I'll ever get used to you not being here!

I just came back from the pool. I kept thinking about last summer when we had that jumping contest off the diving board.

Darren and Carly were at the pool today, too. Carly showed me her new Green Jade Razzle Stone. It's pretty cool. I need the Blue Midnight Stone to get up to the third level, but neither of them wanted to trade their extras with me.

I miss you a lot! Write back soon!

Your best friend,

Josh

T.J. and I used to trade Razzle Stones without ever asking for trade backs. Razzle Stones are special colored stones a lot of kids collect. Some stones are easy to get when you buy a Razzle Bag at the store, but other stones are so rare that almost no one has them. Besides collecting the stones, you can also play games with them.

I asked my mom for a stamp and walked to the mailbox at the end of the street to mail the letter. I passed T.J.'s old house on my way there. Inside the house I could hear a dog barking.

Scott was sitting on the front steps with markers and a big pad on his lap, and it looked like he was drawing something. I know he saw me. Then he stood up and walked back inside his house. He didn't even say hi or anything.

Chapter 2
The New Kid

As the days passed, I wondered when T.J. would get my letter. I thought about him reading it and hoped he would write back right away. Even though I went bike-riding with Carly and did stuff with my other friends, I thought about T.J. a lot. Finally, after a week or so, I got another letter from T.J.

July 30

Dear Josh,

I remember that diving contest very well! I swallowed so much pool water I felt sick for two days!

You're right. I guess it will take a while to get used to being here. They don't have a pool in this town. They don't even have sidewalks on my street! I can't imagine what I'm going to do for the rest of the summer!

Some people down the road invited us to swim in their pool last weekend. They have a six-year-old girl, so Kyle is really happy. Now he has someone to play with. There are no kids my age on this whole block! My mom said she heard there were some kids my age who live around the corner, but they go to camp all summer.

You might ask some other kids to trade Razzle Stones with you. I think Randi has the Blue Midnight Stone. I bet she'd really want your Purple Paw Stone.

Your best friend,

T.J.

The next afternoon the doorbell rang. Darren and Carly were standing outside, wanting to know if I could play basketball at the playground down the street.

"T.J. should be here," Darren said as he dribbled the basketball down the sidewalk. "He shoots hoops almost as well as I do." I thought T.J. was better than Darren, but I didn't say anything.

When we passed T.J.'s old house, I saw Scott and his sister sitting on the front steps.

"Hey!" Darren yelled over to Scott. "Do you play basketball?" I didn't think Darren had met Scott, but Darren talks to everyone.

His older sister, Amanda, stood up. “Sure he does,” she said, giving Scott a nudge. Scott looked startled, but he didn’t say anything.

He didn’t look too excited to play, but he walked over to us. He was taller than I thought.

“Are you coming?” Darren asked.

“OK,” Scott muttered.

At the playground we played two-on-two. Scott and I played together. Scott didn’t seem really interested in the game because he didn’t make one basket. Finally, I got tired of playing and said I wanted to go home.

Darren crowed, “Sore loser! Maybe next time you’ll do better.”

I really didn't like the way Darren was always teasing people. I was already angry about losing the game. Still, I tried to laugh it off and act like I didn't care.

Then Scott said he wanted to go home, too. He quickly said, "Well, see you later," and started to walk home. He didn't even wait to walk with me. Scott is nothing at all like T.J.

August 18

Dear T.J.,

Hi! How are you?

That's too bad there are no kids on your block. Maybe when school starts you'll meet some kids in your new neighborhood. The people who moved into your house have a kid our age, but I really don't play with him. I don't think he likes me. He doesn't seem to like to play basketball, and he doesn't say much.

I'm going to the beach next week to visit my cousins. I love to go to the beach. Did you go on vacation yet? I can't believe school starts in just a few weeks. My mom wants to take me shopping for school supplies and clothes after we get back. I'm not ready for school.

That's about it for now. I miss you a lot. Write soon!

Your best friend,

Josh

Chapter 3
School Starts

After I sent T.J. the last letter, I began to wonder who I would sit with on the school bus. I had always sat next to T.J., but this year he wouldn't be on the bus. I tried playing with my Razzle Stones to keep from thinking about it, but that empty feeling inside me felt stronger than ever.

August 30

Dear Josh,

We never went anywhere for a vacation this summer at all! My parents said it cost too much to move and we'd do something next summer. This was my worst summer ever!

School starts tomorrow here. I hate being the new kid! I wonder who I'll sit next to on the school bus. Remember how you and I always sat together?

I'm bringing in one of my Red Ruby Razzle Stones in my backpack. You know, it's the Lucky Stone. My parents said just to be nice and friendly and listen to the teachers and I should be fine. That's what parents HAVE to say!!

I miss everyone back home, especially you!

Your best friend,
T.J.

On the first day of school I sat on the school bus next to the kid around the corner. He didn't stop talking. He just kept going on and on about how excited he was, what clubs he was going to join, his teacher, his new best friends, and on and on. I don't understand how some people just never stop talking. My mom says I'm too shy sometimes, but I wouldn't want to be a motormouth either!

September 15

Dear T.J.,

Hi! School started here last week. My teacher is Mrs. Jenkins. She seems nice. We're doing a project on volcanoes. Everyone in the class built a volcano, and we let them all erupt at the same time. It was really messy and fun.

A lot of kids brought Razzle Stones to school. Darren was showing off his Diamond Wishing Stone during lunch. Next to the Premium Flash Stone, it's the rarest Razzle Stone in the pyramid. I heard there are only a few Diamond Wishing Stones in the whole country.

Soccer season starts this Saturday. The Kicks won't be the same soccer team without you. Are you on a soccer team in your new town?

That's too bad you never went on vacation this year, but I bet your parents will take you on a really great vacation next summer.

Write soon!

Your best friend,

Josh

September 29

Dear Josh,

Hi! What's up?

Yes, I'm on a soccer team here called the Storms. We had our first game yesterday, and we won 4 to 3. I scored a goal. A kid named Paul also scored a goal. He lives around the corner from me. He's a year older, but he's all right. He introduced me to some other kids, too. There's a girl two blocks away from me who's in the same class as I am.

My teacher's name is Mrs. Murphy. She called me Thomas Jonathan! After I talked to her, she said she would call me T.J., but now some of the other kids are calling me Thomas Jonathan.

I traded my two Amber Gold Stones for the Green Jade Stone. There are a lot of kids here who like to collect and trade Razzle Stones. I can't wait for your next letter!

Your best friend,
T.J. (YES, T.J., NOT
Thomas Jonathan)

The next Saturday morning my team, the Kicks, played our first soccer game. It was a total disaster, and we lost 6 to 1. I wondered if things would have been any better if T.J. had been on our team. He was such a good soccer player.

After the game some of the kids wanted to meet at the playground to trade Razzle Stones. I went home first; then I took about ten of my better stones and put them in my special Razzle Pouch. I put the pouch in my jacket pocket.

I jumped on my bike. Scott and his father were next door washing their car. Scott's father gave me a big smile. "Hi, Josh, what's new?" he asked.

"Nothing really," I said.

"I noticed the other day you collect Razzle Stones. Scott does, too. We have the Razzle Stone board game in the house. Why don't you two play a game?" he said. Scott looked a little embarrassed that his dad was making the invitation.

"Maybe later," I said. "I'm going to meet some kids at the playground to trade stones. Do you have a bike?" I asked Scott. He shook his head and looked down. Scott's dad started to say something, but then stopped. "Later is fine," Scott's dad said.

"OK," I said, and rode off on my bike. If I had the Diamond Wishing Stone, I would have wished that T.J. still lived next door to me instead of Scott.

I thought I was going to be late, so I raced down the street, pedaling hard. When I reached the playground a few blocks away, there was a group of kids by the tall trees at the far side of the park. I rode down the hill, passed the basketball court, the swings, and the pond. I parked my bike and joined the other kids; then I reached into my pocket to get my Razzle Pouch. I checked the other pocket. My pockets were empty!

The Big Loss

I couldn't believe it. I pushed my hands down into both pockets of my jacket. I looked down at the ground. Where could the stones have gone? I began to panic.

"So, Josh, what kind of stones do you have?" Darren asked. He was polishing his Diamond Wishing Stone and barely looked at me.

"I . . . I . . . ," I stammered. "I can't find them. They were right in my pocket!" Everyone looked at me.

Carly asked, "When was the last time you saw them?"

"Just before I left my house, I put them in my pouch, and I put the pouch in my pocket," I said. "They could have fallen out anywhere!"

Some kids looked around with me, but the pouch wasn't anywhere. "I'm going back to look for it," I said as I jumped on my bike.

"We'll wait for you here," Carly called out to me as I rode away.

I rode my bike back through the park, trying to remember the exact path I had ridden. I kept looking down at the ground and almost hit a parked car, but I didn't see the pouch.

I left the park and rode slowly up the street. When I got closer to home, I saw that Scott and his father were still outside.

"Did you see a pouch with Razzle Stones inside it?" I asked them. "It was in my pocket, but it must have fallen out. I can't find it anywhere."

Scott and his father looked around on the sidewalk and in their driveway, even under the car. They didn't see anything.

"Which stones did you have with you?" Scott asked. These were more words at one time than I had ever heard from him.

I started to name them, "The Green Jade, Coal Black, Sun Fire . . ." but stopped. From their expressions, I knew that Scott and his father hadn't seen my Razzle Stones.

"Sorry," said Scott's father, "I don't think you dropped them here."

I walked inside my house, feeling like there was a big hole in my stomach. I went into my bedroom and looked at my stone pyramid. I had only seven Razzle Stones on the pyramid steps, and they were all at the bottom of the pyramid, the stones that were the most common. I had been collecting stones since last spring, and now almost my whole Razzle Stone collection was gone.

I told my mom, and she said she'd walk back to the playground with me and look. We walked slowly there and back, searching everywhere. My Razzle Stones weren't anywhere. We'd either missed seeing the pouch or someone had picked it up and taken it.

October 14

Dear T.J.,

Hi! I had an awful week. I lost my pouch with my best Razzle Stones in it. I bought another bag with some allowance money, but when I looked inside, there were just some ordinary stones, not any of the really good rare stones. My mom promised she'd buy me a new bag this weekend. Now I'll have to start building up my collection all over again.

Everything else is pretty much the same. Whenever I see your house, I still can't believe you're not living there. The new kid who moved into your house is in my class, but he never says much. I don't know what's wrong with him.

Well, that's about it for now. Write back soon. (Who is Thomas Jonathan? Just kidding.)

Your best friend,

Josh

I mailed the letter on a Friday and got a letter back from T.J. the next Wednesday. I couldn't believe he had written and sent the letter so fast. I felt something small and hard inside the envelope. What could it be?

Chapter 5

Trying Harder

I opened the letter carefully. A Sun Fire Stone fell out into my hand! It shone bright yellow, and when I held it up to the light, the stone sparkled even more. T.J. was the best friend ever! I hurried into my bedroom and placed the stone on the fourth level of my pyramid. My pyramid of stones was slowly starting to grow again. Then I read the letter.

October 19

Dear Josh,

I'm sorry you lost your best Razzle Stones, but here's a Sun Fire to help you build up your stone collection again.

I went pumpkin picking this past weekend. There was a hayride and a cornstalk maze. It was a lot of fun. The weather up here is really getting cold. Today it was almost freezing outside.

I'm going to be a clown for Halloween. I have a silly wig, baggy pants, and big shoes. What are you going to be?

I don't know what's wrong with your new neighbor. I do know it's tough being the new kid when you don't know anyone, and all the kids around you have known each other forever. Maybe he's just shy. One thing I know for sure; I feel better now that I've made some friends.

Write soon!

Your best friend,

T.J.

After school the next day, I wanted to get home to write T.J. a letter. When I got off the bus, I started walking home with Carly. Scott walked ahead of us, alone as usual.

After we got to Carly's house, I looked ahead at Scott. I remembered what T.J. had said about how hard it was to be the new kid. I was glad I didn't have to move to a new town.

I began to think that it really must be hard for Scott, too. I didn't know what town he had moved from. I had never asked. Maybe it was really different from this town. Still, Scott never really talked much to anyone. I never really talked to him either, so maybe it was time for me to do something about it. I walked a little faster.

As I came up behind Scott I said, "That school science show was funny, don't you think?"

Scott turned to me with a surprised look on his face. "Yeah, I guess," he said.

Neither of us said anything more as we continued walking. A couple of minutes later, I finally said, "You want to come over to my house after you finish your homework?"

Scott stared at me for a few seconds, then said, "OK." He seemed to relax a little.

We walked in silence again until I finally reached my house. I turned to walk up the driveway and said to Scott, "See you later."

"Yeah," Scott replied, and for the first time since I had met him, Scott smiled.

About 4:30 P.M., my doorbell rang. It was Scott. We decided to play a soccer game on my family's computer. Scott wasn't very quick at first, so I played with him on an easy level. He became really excited when he started scoring goals.

"This is great!" he said.

I laughed, then asked, "Do you have a computer at your house?"

He nodded. "We just got it a couple of months ago. We don't have this game, though," he said.

When it was almost 6 P.M., Mom asked Scott if he'd like to stay for dinner.

"Yes," he said, smiling, but then he frowned. "I can't," he said softly. "I've got something I have to do. May I come tomorrow?"

"Of course you may," my mom said.

I wondered what Scott had to do, but I didn't ask. He didn't seem as if he wanted to talk about it.

The next day was Friday, and our teacher announced a special no-homework weekend. That meant Scott and I could start playing right after school. We went to my house first, and Scott asked if we could play the computer game again.

After we started playing, I saw he was having such a good time I told him he could borrow the game to take home. His whole face lit up. "Cool!" he said.

It was still early, so we went over to his house. When we got to the door, a big happy dog jumped all over me and licked my face. Scott said the dog's name was Grizwald. He showed me how he had taught Grizwald to roll over; then he snapped his fingers and Grizwald stood up on his hind legs. He was a really smart dog.

We went up to Scott's room to play the Razzle Stone board game. He asked me if I had ever found the stones I had lost. I said no, and then told him about T.J. sending me a Sun Fire Stone.

When I walked into Scott's room, I saw a lot of drawings hanging on the wall. On his desk, Scott had another drawing. It looked just like our street, with the houses and the fire station on the corner. Even the street signs were exactly like those on our block, although some of the letters were reversed.

"Did you draw this?" I asked. Scott nodded.

"It's great. It looks so real!" I exclaimed.

Then I saw IT.

There, right on Scott's dresser, was his Razzle Stone pyramid. On the very top of the pyramid was Premium Flash, the biggest, rarest Razzle Stone there was! A rainbow of colors glittered from every angle. Premium Flash sparkled brighter than all the other stones.

I was excited. “When did you get Premium Flash?” I asked, almost in a whisper.

“It was about two weeks ago,” he said. “I almost fell over when I opened the bag and there it was at the bottom of the sand.”

He took the stone off the pyramid and handed it to me. The stone felt heavy in the palm of my hand.

“You can borrow it, if you want,” he said.

I couldn’t believe it. “Really?” I asked doubtfully. Once you get a Premium Flash stone you’re never supposed to let it out of your sight.

"Really," Scott said. "I know you'll take good care of it."

I held the stone tightly in my hand. "Thanks! I'll bring it back tomorrow," I said.

"No rush," he replied and smiled.

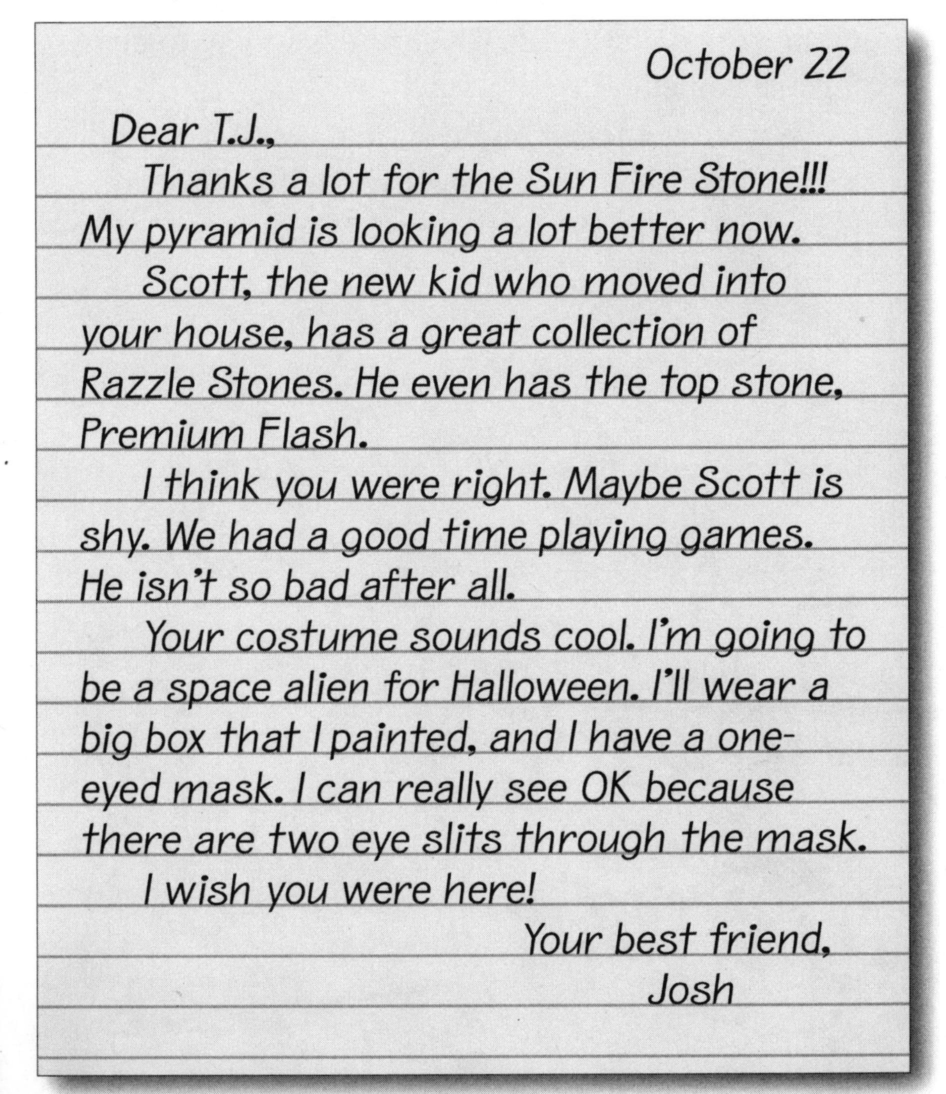

October 22

Dear T.J.,

Thanks a lot for the Sun Fire Stone!!! My pyramid is looking a lot better now.

Scott, the new kid who moved into your house, has a great collection of Razzle Stones. He even has the top stone, Premium Flash.

I think you were right. Maybe Scott is shy. We had a good time playing games. He isn't so bad after all.

Your costume sounds cool. I'm going to be a space alien for Halloween. I'll wear a big box that I painted, and I have a one-eyed mask. I can really see OK because there are two eye slits through the mask.

I wish you were here!

Your best friend,

Josh

A few days later it was finally Halloween. I went trick-or-treating with some kids from the neighborhood and asked Scott to come, too. He was dressed like a Granger football player, with a helmet, uniform, and shoulder pads. I told him about T.J. and how his parents had taken us to a Granger game last year. Scott said he'd like to go to a game someday.

We were out for a couple of hours until it started to get dark. Then Scott came over to my house to play for a while. We had a good time.

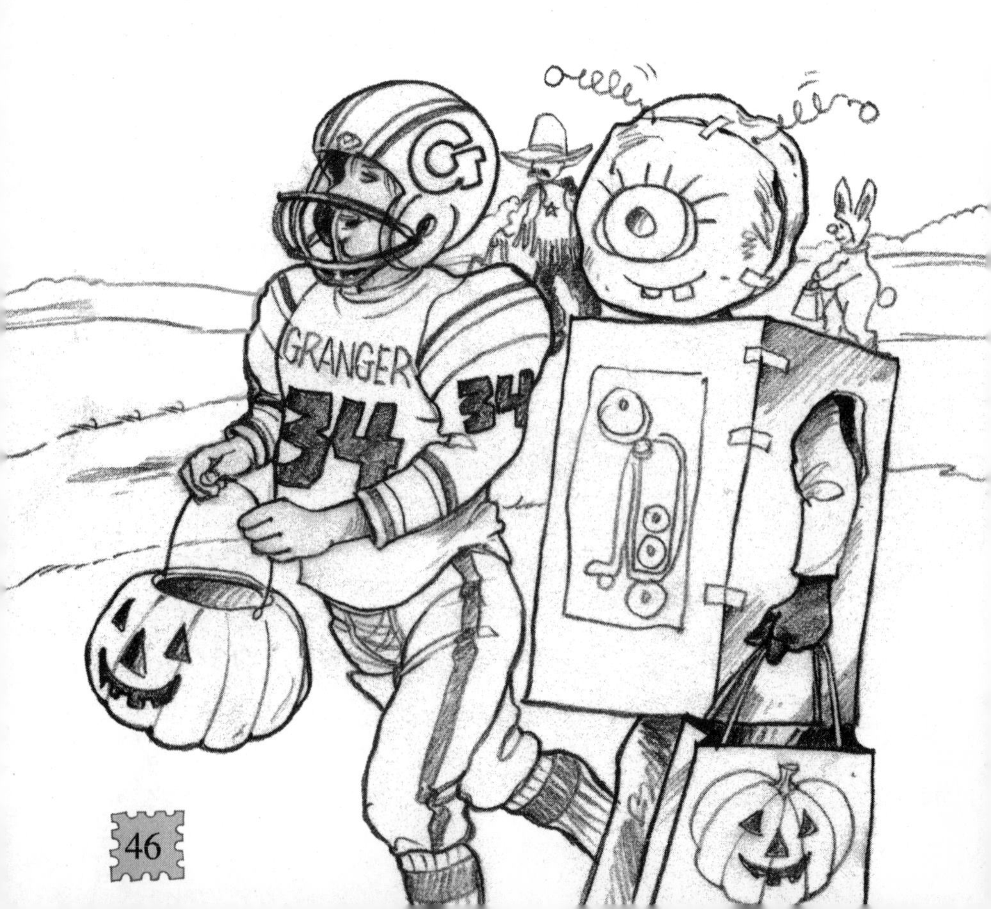

The Saturday after Halloween was so warm and sunny, it almost felt like summer again. My mom even let me go outside in a T-shirt and no jacket. I was with Scott when a group of kids came riding past on their bikes. Carly stopped."We're going to the playground," she said. "Darren has the new Razzle Stone card game. Do you want to come?"

"Sure!" I said and looked at Scott. He didn't look like he really wanted to go. Then I remembered that he didn't have a bike.

"Do you want to walk over with me?" I asked him. Scott nodded, although he still didn't say anything. We walked to the playground after the other kids rode off on their bikes.

When we got to the park, there must have been ten kids surrounding Darren. They were all sitting together, and Darren was handing out cards to everyone. On each of the cards was a Razzle Stone picture with instructions on how to use the stone in the game.

Each of us took a turn picking a card and reading it out loud. When Scott picked up a card, he stumbled on the words. He tried reading the instructions, but he was so slow. He sighed hard.

"What's WRONG with you?" Darren barked. "Can't you read?"

Scott just looked down. He didn't say anything, then threw the card he was holding on the ground.

"Forget it!" Scott said. He quickly stood up and began walking out of the park.

"What's his problem?" Darren said.

I looked at Scott, hurrying out of the park. This time I wasn't going to ignore it, so I stood up and ran after him.

Chapter 7
Seeing Backwards

"Wait!" I called to Scott. Scott was walking really fast, almost running away.

"Darren has a big mouth," I said breathlessly as I caught up to Scott.

"I don't care!" Scott said angrily. He kicked at some leaves on the sidewalk.

I wasn't sure what to say.

Scott walked faster and looked down at the sidewalk. When he got to his house, he ran inside.

The next day I saw Scott's sister Amanda. When I said hello, she ignored me at first. Then she turned and stared at me. She said, "You know, I think you were mean to my brother."

"What do you mean?" I asked. I had no idea what she was talking about.

"Just because Scott isn't as quick to read as you and your friends are," she replied.

"That was Darren," I said. "I never said anything to Scott."

Amanda put her hands on her hips. "Scott has a learning disability," she said suddenly. Then she looked down. "You probably wouldn't understand, anyway."

"What are you talking about? What is a learning disability?" I asked.

Amanda looked at me. "The doctor says it's something he was born with. He has a hard time reading, and sometimes he sees letters backwards. When he was little, some sports were difficult for him too, like riding a bike and playing basketball. It's hard to explain. Wait a minute."

Amanda ran back inside her house and brought out a book. She turned to a picture and showed it to me. "Here," she said, "can you read this?"

I looked at the print on the page. The letters looked backwards. "How could you expect me to read this?" I asked.

"That's how Scott sees words sometimes. He can't help it." Amanda told me. "A lot of kids have other kinds of learning disabilities. Some people just think the kids are stupid and call them names."

Then I remembered Scott's drawings and how some letters were reversed on the street signs.

"He's really good at drawing," I said slowly.

"That's how it is with learning disabilities," Amanda explained. "Some kids do really well in some things and other kids do really well in others. Scott has a talent for art and music. It's just like kids without learning disabilities. Everybody's different."

I nodded. I guess I didn't know Scott as well as I thought. I did know that I was glad we were friends.

When I saw Scott at school the next morning, I wasn't sure if I should tell him what Amanda said. I wasn't even sure if he would talk to me after what had happened at the playground.

I thought he was about to pass me in the hall without saying anything. Then he came up to me. "I heard what my sister said to you," he said. "I don't know why she does that."

"That's OK," I said. "I never knew some people see words backwards."

"I take special classes," Scott said. "That's why I couldn't stay for dinner. It really helps, but I still can't read very fast. I have to concentrate. I used to have trouble riding a bike, too, although I'm much better now. My dad said I need a bigger bike because I outgrew my old one."

I asked Scott, "Do you want to come over to my house after school?"

"Sure!" he said. "Great!"

"We'd better get to class," I said. "The bell about to ring."

We walked to class together. I was glad to see that he was smiling. I was smiling, too.

Chapter 8
The Great Surprise

November 15

Dear Josh,

Hi! Guess what? My parents just told me we're going to visit my aunt back in our old town for the Thanksgiving weekend. They said we might be able to stop and visit you.

I'm so excited! I can't wait to see you and the old neighborhood. Please, please write back and tell me you'll be around that weekend.

Your best friend,
T.J.

I ran to ask my mom about Thanksgiving. She said we would be going to my grandparents on Thanksgiving Day, but we would be home the rest of the weekend. I ran back to my room to write T.J. a letter right away. This was so great.

November 18

Dear T.J.,

That's GREAT that you're coming here! My mom said we're going to be here the day after Thanksgiving and the rest of the weekend. I can't wait to see you!

Your best friend,

Josh

The day after Thanksgiving, the doorbell rang. I ran to open the door. T.J., his brother Kyle, and his parents were outside.

"Teej!" I said. T.J. looked exactly the same, even though I hadn't seen him in five months.

"Josh-oo-ah," he called out like he used to. We both laughed.

Mom asked T.J.'s family to come in. She asked them about their new house and their move. They said it had taken a while to get settled in, but they really liked the new place now.

While my mom and T.J.'s parents talked, T.J. and I went to my room. Kyle tagged along, too.

After about an hour, my mom called us back to the kitchen. She said, "T.J.'s parents and I wonder if you two would like to have a sleepover here tonight. They'll pick up T.J. tomorrow afternoon."

T.J. and I looked at each other. "Yes!" we shouted. "Way to go!"

T.J. and I had a great time together. We played outside, then played some video and computer games indoors. We talked about school and the kids T.J. used to know. He asked about the people next door, and I told him about Scott. I said they were away for the holiday, but they might be back before T.J. had to leave.

Mom let us have pizza for dinner. Then we made popcorn and watched a movie on TV. We stayed up until midnight. It almost felt like T.J. had never moved away.

The next day after breakfast, the doorbell rang. It was Scott.

"Hi," he said. "We're back, so I was wondering if you could play."

"My friend T.J. is here," I told him.

T.J. came to the door. "Josh told me about you," he said. "I hoped I'd get to meet you."

"Are you the one who used to live in my house?" Scott asked him.

"That's me!" T.J. said.

"You want to come in?" I asked Scott.

He hesitated for a moment. Then he said, "Sure," and came in.

The three of us went to my room and played the Razzle Stone board game that Scott had brought. Then we went into the kitchen for some juice.

As we sat at the kitchen table, T.J. asked Scott, "Do you like living here?"

“It took a while to get used to it,” Scott said. “I came from a big city. This place is a lot smaller.”

“It took me a while to get used to my new house and neighborhood, too,” T.J. said. “It’s hard being the new kid.”

“It is hard,” Scott sighed. Then he looked over at me. “It helps when you make a really good friend,” he said.

It sure does help to make a good friend, I thought, and I never even had to move.

Then we talked about Razzle Stones for a while. Scott ran home to bring over his collection of stones to show T.J.

Scott and T.J. had stones that were much rarer than the ones I had. I was still building up my collection after I had lost my stones at the park.

Even though I didn't have as many Razzle Stones as they did, it didn't bother me. As I sat there with my two best friends, one old and one new, I felt really lucky and special in a different way. That kind of feeling I can never lose.

Glossary

adjust	[uh JUST] to get used to one's surroundings
disability	[dihs uh BIHL uh tee] the condition of not being able or fit to do something
dribbled	[DRIHB uld] used short bounces to move a basketball
expressions	[eks PRESH unz] ways that the face looks that shows how one feels
instructions	[ihn STRUK shunz] orders or directions, such as the directions that tell how to play a game
miserable	[MIHZ ur uh bul] very unhappy or sad
practically	[PRAK tihk lee] almost, nearly
rare	[rair] not often found or seen
reversed	[ree VURST] turned around; backwards
talent	[TAL unt] a natural skill that is unusual